dedicated to Dick Robinson,

who has inspired word collectors worldwide.

—P.H.R.

Library of Congress Cataloging-in-Publication Data available

ISBN 978-0-545-86502-9

10 9 8 7 6 5 4 3 2 1   18 19 20 21 22

Printed in China 38 • First edition, February 2018

The text type and display are hand-lettered by Peter H. Reynolds.

Reynolds Studio assistance by Julia Anne Young • Book design by Patti Ann Harris

the Word Collector

PETER HAMILTON REYNOLDS

ORCHARD BOOKS

AN IMPRINT of SCHOLASTIC INC.

Collectors collect things...

Some people collect stamps.

Some people collect coins.

Others collect rocks.

Some collect art.

Some collect bugs.

Others collect baseball cards.

Some people collect comic books.

And Jerome?
What did
HE
collect?

Jerome collected words.

He collected words he
heard.

Certain words caught his attention.

He collected words he **saw.**

WILLOW

WILLOW
TEA SHOPPE

Certain words jumped out at him.

He collected words he
read.

Certain words popped off the page.

Short and sweet words.

Two-syllable treats.

And multi-syllable words that
sounded like little songs.

There were words he did not know the
meaning of at first, but they were

marvelous

to say.

There were words whose sounds
were perfectly suited to their meaning.

Jerome filled his scrapbooks with
more and more
of his favorite words.

Jerome's collections grew. He began organizing them.
"DREAMY" "SCIENCE" "SAD" "ACTION" "POETIC"
One day, while transporting them—

Jerome slipped and
his words went
flying!

As he began to pick them up, he noticed
his collections had become
jumbled.

Big words next to little words.
Sad words next to dreamy words.

Jerome began stringing words **together.**

Words he had not imagined being
side by side.

He used his words
to write poems.

He used his poems to make songs.

They moved. They delighted.

Some of his simplest words were his most

powerful.

Jerome eagerly collected
more and more
of his favorite words.

The more words he knew the more
clearly he could share with the world
what he was thinking, feeling, and dreaming.

One breezy afternoon,
Jerome climbed the highest hill,
pulling a wagon packed with
his word collection.

He smiled as he
emptied his collection of words
into the wind.

He saw children in the valley below...

...scurrying about collecting words from the breeze.

Jerome
had no words
to describe how happy
that made him.

REACH FOR YOUR OWN WORDS

TELL THE WORLD WHO YOU ARE

AND HOW YOU WILL MAKE IT BETTER

—PETER HAMILTON REYNOLDS